DINOSAURS DON'T HAVE BEDTIMES!
GRRR!

To Freddy and Lily,
with love
T.K.

For my beautiful big sister Sarah,
who can only dream of sleep
N.D.

First published 2016 by Walker Books Ltd, 87 Vauxhall Walk, London SE11 5HJ · Text © 2016 Timothy Knapman 10 9 8 7 6 5 4 3 2 1
Illustrations © 2016 Nikki Dyson · The right of Timothy Knapman and Nikki Dyson to be identified as author and illustrator respectively of this work has been asserted by them in accordance with the Copyright, Designs and Patents Act 1988 · This book has been typeset in Chowderhead and Billy · Printed in China · British Library Cataloguing in Publication Data: a catalogue record for this book is available from the British Library · ISBN 978-1-4063-4191-1 (hardback)
ISBN 978-1-4063-7219-9 (paperback) · www.walker.co.uk

DINOSAURS DON'T HAVE BEDTIMES!

Timothy Knapman illustrated by Nikki Dyson

"Suppertime!" said Mummy.

"But dinosaurs don't HAVE suppertimes!" said Mo.

"Really?" said Mummy.
"They must get very hungry."
"They eat whenever they like," said Mo.

GOBBLE, GOBBLE,
CRUNCH!

"And do they ALWAYS make a dreadful mess?"

"YES!"

"Bath time!" said Mummy.

"But dinosaurs don't HAVE bath times!" said Mo.

"They must have dirty ears!" said Mummy.

"Yes!" said Mo.

"They roll around in the swampy water.

They do not scrub beneath their claws.

They don't put toothpaste on their jaws.

They don't WANT to be clean and shiny!"

"Towel!"

"GROWL!"
SOAP

"Pyjama time!" said Mummy.

"But dinosaurs don't WEAR pyjamas!" said Mo.

“Where would their tails go?
They must get very cold!” said Mummy.

“Dinosaurs don’t care!”

“Just the bottoms then,” said Mummy.

“That is NOT fair!”

HMPH!

"Play time!" said Mummy.

"Dinosaurs don't play nicely!" said Mo.

GRRRRR!
GRRRR!

"They're much too big for that!
They wriggle and they run
and they hide inside the jungle ...
for days and days sometimes...
Then they jump out, SHOUTING!
Now, THAT'S dinosaur fun!"

YARL!

"Milk time!" said Mummy.

"Dinosaurs DON'T drink their milk," said Mo.

"Dinosaurs rampage!
They stomp around and
knock things down!"

BASH!
GROWL!
HOWL!

Yaaaaawn!

"Bedtime!" said Mummy.

"Dinosaurs DON'T have bedtimes!" said Mo.

"They're never, ever tired."

"Don't they ever, ever sleep?"

"No!"

ROAR!

"But sometimes..." Mo yawned.
"They might just close their eyes.
And curl up tight and snuggle down...
But all of that's pretend."

"And do they have a night-night kiss?"
said Mummy.

"Roar! Roar!"

ROARrrr

"Goodnight, dinosaur."